SHORT AND SWEET

VOLUME TWO

Edited by
Liane McKay

SOOR PLOOM
PRESS

First published 2023 by Soor Ploom Press
Tulligarth Park
Alloa
Scotland, UK.

soorploompress.com

ISBN: 978-1-7396284-1-3

Cover photo by Brecht Deboosere.
Designed and typeset by Liane McKay.
Printed in the UK by Imprint Digital Ltd.

Contents

Introduction   9

Body and Sensation   11

Capacity   13
Joanna Helms

Faltering   14
May Sharpe

White Spirit (an extract from Chapter 2)   15
Carol McKay

Weathering Is What I Would Like to Do Well   17
Anjali Ramayya

Witches of the Central Belt III: A Visitor   18
Jenny Munro-Hunt

Vengeance   19
Lesley Jane Black

Cassandra   20
Karen Arnold

Cat and Mouse   22
Helen Chambers

Green & Black's   24
Ben Banyard

Ragnarök Postponed   25
Tavia Allan

I Have Trust Issues with the Weather   27
Eileen Farrelly

Dawn Chorus   28
NL Whiteley

A Study of Anguish   29
Morag Anderson

My Best Friend   30
Catherine McKinlay

Shape and Movement   31

Dance of the Midges   33
Nikita Parik

Threat of the Urban Reds   34
Beth McDonough

Little Poems   35
Donald Saunders

But No Ladies   36
Annie Sturgeon

Rising Skylark Sings   37
Annie Sturgeon

Cardinal Wooing   38
Salvatore Difalco

Last Sleepy Half Thoughts Before Sleep   39
Bruach Mhor

How to Call Geese   40
Paulette Dubé

Hivernal (Winter in Montreal)   41
Alison Roe

Haiku for Hire   42
Michael McGill

Abhainn Shira   43
Martin Goldie

Cause and Effect   44
Andy Raffan

Connection and Memory   45

The Playground   47
Emily Tee

Lost-and-Found   48
Sean McMenemy

Child   49
Allan Gaw

Paper Crowns   50
Claire Reynolds

A Teenage New Year in Wales   52
Jim Lloyd

Send Me a Postcard   53
Eileen Farrelly

Things We Miss As Parents   54
Ben Banyard

Good Ol' Mom and Pop   55
Darrell Petska

Nae Sae Different   56
Eilidh Crofton

Japanese Visitor   58
Charlie Gracie

Time   59
Katy Ewing

Transformation and Belief   61

Blossoming   63
Janet Crawford

Bluebells   64
Ian McDonough

A Trick of the Dappled Light   65
Ellen Forkin

When Death Comes Calling   66
Lyndsey Croal

Takeaway Mourning   68
John Tinney

Erosion   70
Andy Raffan

For Sale: Childhood Memories   71
Liane McKay

Cash or Card?   72
Karen Arnold

A Sting in the Tale   74
Kate Leimer

Months Go By   76
Liane McKay

The Stacks   77
Scott Montgomery

Ghost in the Machine   79
Hilary Ayshford

Gorleston Gulls   81
Laura Lewis-Waters

Sunweys and Widdershins   82
Hilary Coyne

Acknowledgements   85

Author biographies   86

A note on Shannon Trust   93

Editor's note: Where a piece uses a language other than British English (e.g. American English, Scots), the author's original spellings are retained.

Introduction

The second volume of *Short and Sweet* collects more great pieces of short fiction and poetry – lovingly termed 'Plooms' at Soor Ploom Press HQ – authored by writers from around the world. As before, you might come across some Scots pieces in these pages, which I hope you'll enjoy. This publishing press is, after all, named in Scots after a Scottish sweetie held dear by many – especially me!

Short as ever, Volume Two promises no frills, no fuss – just works that aim to resonate with the human experience. Each piece distills the essence of life's most ordinary – and extraordinary – moments into 500 words or less. The chapters are not rigid; they serve loosely as a guide to some of the themes running through these works, without being prescriptive one way or the other. Many of the Plooms in this book cross boundaries, inviting us to see things differently.

In our first chapter, **Body and Sensation**, we take a close-up lens to our physical selves, looking keenly at our bodies. We see how they can be powerful, as in Karen Arnold's *Cassandra*, but also unsettling, like in Joanna Helms' *Capacity*. We explore our senses in works by Helen Chambers, Ben Banyard, NL Whiteley and Catherine McKinlay, while Jenny Munro-Hunt gives us a playfully gruesome love poem in *Witches of the Central Belt III: A Visitor*.

Shape and Movement expands on this zoomed-in view by taking us outside to the natural world. We see wit in poems by Beth McDonough and Donald Saunders, and an entertaining snapshot of romance in Salvatore Difalco's *Cardinal Wooing*, while Martin Goldie brings still landscapes to life in *Abhainn Shira*.

The third chapter, **Connection and Memory**, celebrates our ties to the people and places of our lives, both past and present. Eilidh Crofton's *Nae Sae Different* and Charlie Gracie's *Japanese Visitor* remind us that we may all have more in common than we think. Sean McMenemy delivers a poignant and multi-layered flash fiction in *Lost-and-Found*, while a tender poem by Allan Gaw balances Jim Lloyd's humorous story of teenage mischief.

Finally, we move into a realm of **Transformation and Belief**, exploring mystery and intrigue in pieces by Hilary Ayshford, Scott Montgomery and Laura Lewis-Waters. Difficult feelings melt away in intimate poems by Andy Raffan and Janet Crawford, while Hilary Coyne investigates what happens when we upset the balance of things in *Sunweys and Widdershins*.

In Volume Two, expect moments of stillness and fluidity; clarity and thoughtfulness; humour and emotion. There's no need to read the whole book at once – although you're more than welcome to! This is a collection to revisit regularly. I invite you to savour this new batch of Plooms in your pockets of free time, creating moments just like the pieces in this book – short and sweet.

Liane McKay

Body and Sensation

You smile in the mirror,
trace the stretch marks on your belly,
the tapestry of stitches
pricked into the finest suture line

Anjali Ramayya, *Weathering Is What I Would Like to Do Well*

Capacity

Joanna Helms

sometimes it feels limitless,

a well of unknown depth and resource.

other times,

I feel a long fingernail

press

on the soft of my heart,

which bubbles weakly,

like a damp sponge.

Faltering

May Sharpe

Drip tap
Tick clock
Heart beat
Drip tap
Beep chirp
Heart beat
Tap tick
Clock beep
Tick drip
Heart beat
Drip tap
Tick clock
Heart

White Spirit (an extract from Chapter 2)

Carol McKay

They could see the blue lights cycling through their sequence ahead of them. Allan MacIntyre pulled his Alfa to the verge behind the uniform car and he and Jane Coburn got out. It was a typical day in early autumn. The birch leaves were yellowing on the hillside, yet the pasture was green, all the way down and across the wide valley. With the sky clear, Loch Ness below them pooled still and deep, and deep blue. Back on the hillside, it hadn't rained for weeks, so the ground was dry and the copper and yellow leaves that had already fallen crumpled under their feet.

'What a place to die,' Allan said. A look passed between them. 'I never get used to this bit.' Hands on his hips, Allan breathed in lungfuls of fresh air as they waited while the first responder approached them.

'Hello, Sir. Ma'am. It's the body of a young male – just a boy, really – half-way up the hill in the thick of the woodland. Age about thirteen? Looks recent. The elderly woman who found him's a bit shocked.' He nodded his head towards the second police car. 'Do you want to go and speak to her first, or see the body?'

'We'll look at the scene.'

The PC held his arm out to indicate the direction then led Allan and Jane across the single track road, over a narrow draining ditch clogged with yellowed grasses and thistles festooned with fuzzy seed heads.

The route was steep and full of tussocks. Grasses were bent aside and some of the mossy patches were smeared with foot falls – plenty of signs of someone passing in a hurry.

He looked uphill to the young policeman. 'Is it much further?'

'About the same again?'

'Jesus.' He searched in his pockets for a bar of tablet and broke off two squares. 'Want a bit?' he asked the others. The PC shook his head. Jane accepted.

'Tablet?' There was a note of disbelief in her voice. The sweetie was basically sugar melted in milk with a vanilla pod waved over it.

'Need a wee sugar buzz to help me tackle this mountain.'

'Ah, southern softies!'

'Aye, they don't have terrain like this in Balornock.'

It was battlefield humour. Funny how the mood changed as they drew closer. Allan could tell they were near by the way the PC slowed down and his movements became more reverential. He talked less, with eventually a quiet, 'Just up ahead, Sir,' before shoving aside some thick fronds of juniper to let the DI in to the small clear patch where the body had been found.

Weathering Is What I Would Like to Do Well

after Alastair Reid

Anjali Ramayya

You smile in the mirror,
trace the stretch marks on your belly,
the tapestry of stitches
pricked into the finest suture line.
Who knew, you say,
you who always hated to sew,
who knew that one day
I would become the silk.

Witches of the Central Belt III: A Visitor

Jenny Munro-Hunt

That hangnail –
could I bite it off for you?
or a bit of your arm hair?
would you give me one of your fillings, and then a kiss,
just a wee kiss?
I don't need much and I'll tend to it
so well, I'll bury it
in the bog. This is all I need.
This is all I need
to grow another
and I won't have to bother you again.
I suppose you hear this all the time but
aren't you just glorious?

Vengeance

Lesley Jane Black

Silver sharpness slices
wrinkled greenness.
Small slivers of pickled chartreuse
adorn the plate.
As the knife pushes through
she thinks of things taken
from her
without permission
and feels a satisfaction rarely achieved.

Cassandra

Karen Arnold

The policeman asks me why I have done this. I try to explain that it was because I dreamed of swallows. That in my dream they did not return. And that when I woke, drenched in terror, I knew I had to do something. He does not understand.

I want to hold his bewildered, boyish face between my hands, look into his eyes and explain. This is an emergency, the planet is on fire – but I cannot lift my hands.

The glue is cold and runny when the girl spreads it onto my palm. The feel of it, her tender concern as she applies it, excavates memories of a hospital room, years ago. Ultrasounds at twelve, twenty, thirty weeks when they thought you were not growing, when they feared there was not enough fluid for you to move in. I press my hand to the cold dinosaur body of the digger. She chains herself to an axle.

Water drips from the leaves of ancient oak trees. A blackbird sends up bubbling fountains of song into the grey dawn, while men in acid yellow raincoats watch us from a distance. A glossy woman in make up too perfect for the hour speaks into a microphone. We have become an event, a motley collection of augurs and sibyls.

The sun is rising higher now, air currents form and swirl, pale clouds of insects rise from the wet grass. The police boy asks what will this achieve? Nothing. Something. Everything. He does not understand, and I want to scream as loudly as my missing swallow.

The police boy tries again: why are you doing this?

To slow the fires. To save enough water for you to move in.

He does not understand. They send for bolt cutters and solvents.

Cat and Mouse

Helen Chambers

This relationship needs a touch of magic, you say. So when your back is turned, I sprinkle flour down the gap beside the cooker. Next, I add a dash of mixed spice and finally a gloop of olive oil to clump the grains.

You turn back in time to see me upset a packet of rice. 'Clumsy,' you frown, green eyes flashing, when the peas and lentils I've been weighing skitter like marbles across the floor. Some I swish beneath the cooker when sweeping up. Variety, as you say, is the spice of life. All day, I add food fragments. Biscuit crumbs, fish batter, shavings of crisps. Especially crisps.

When I scamper down at night, my specially prepared larder will sustain me until dawn.

The magic happens while you sleep. My metamorphosis requires concentration and focus. The freedom of my new form excites me, as does keeping it secret from you. My only difficulty is the hunger pangs which grip my gut, the downside to being so tiny. Foraging for leftovers isn't easy in your spotless house.

Tonight, a tempting smell tickles my nostrils from across the kitchen, and I can't resist the lure of a sweating cheese cube. A squeal of delight escapes my careless mouth.

When you flash on the lights on, I become myself at once. Standing full height in the kitchen, a mouse-trap wire bites into my fingers and I blink in pain and shock.

'I set that trap,' you explain, gently unhinging it from my damaged fingers, and holding my hand under cold water. 'I thought we had mice.'

Beside the sink is a saucer with a thin skin of milk. I peer at it, then at you.

When you smile, a bead of milk glistens on your chin.

Green & Black's

Ben Banyard

Look,
I've found this slab
of Christmas chocolate
which I hid
and forgot about.

I'm gently easing my finger
under the paper,
under the thin, thin foil
and now I can really smell it,
bitter and dark.

Would you like a bit?

Ragnarök Postponed

Tavia Allan

Fenrir the Wolf stalks into a greasy spoon on Kilburn High Road.

A young woman is counting her child's toes at the table nearest the door. An old man in a dark coat is reading a folded paper. Neither of them looks at the wolf. He addresses the shiny-faced man behind the counter.

'My name is Hunger.'

'Know what you mean, mate,' says the man. 'Hangover special, is it? Two fried, two sausage, two bacon, black pudding, beans, mushrooms, hash browns, and grilled tomatoes.'

He wipes up the drool that drips from the wolf's mouth and takes that as a yes.

'One double everything!' he calls into the curtain behind him.

'I am Hunger,' growls Fenrir. 'I am Thirst.'

A woman with pink hair emerges from the back. 'Mug of tea, love? Or would you like an iced latte?' She strokes a gleaming contraption. 'We just got a machine.'

'Nah, full-fat Coke's what he needs,' her partner says. He takes a can from the fridge behind him and pops it open.

The wolf slurps the bubbly, sweet, icy liquid and is transported. Never in a thousand, thousand years had he imagined such deliciousness.

Balancing the can between his forepaws, he pads to a table.

'This little piggy had roast beef,' the young mother chants. Her child squeals with delight.

'I will devour you all,' says Fenrir. No one seems to hear, and before he can repeat himself more loudly, the pink-haired woman places a dish before him. The scent drives all other thoughts away.

The eggs and the pig products he recognises. And the mushrooms, which he pushes to one side with his nose. He has no need of visions today. But what are the small things in the golden sauce, and the red things? He sniffs. The smell reminds him of belladonna.

'Tomatoes are good for hangovers,' the old man in the dark coat says. 'Restore your potassium levels. Or something.'

The wolf looks at him. I could open my jaws and swallow you whole, he thinks.

'Don't mind me, son,' says the old man. 'We've all been there.' He returns to his paper.

Fenrir sucks down the eggs and sausages and bacon and blood pudding. He licks up the beans and crunches the hash browns – which are a little overdone. He leaves the hallucinogens uneaten and finishes the Coke.

'Anything else, love?' asks the pink-haired woman, taking his dirty plate.

'I remember when this was all forest,' says Fenrir.

'Ah, well, that's gentrification for you. You know they've started calling this area North Maida Vale?'

'Ridiculous,' the old man agrees.

Fenrir drops several golden coins onto the table, and leaves.

The domed roof of the Black Lion gleams red gold in the sunshine as he lopes up the High Road.

I Have Trust Issues with the Weather

Eileen Farrelly

I grow cynical in spring
increasingly suspicious with each rising degree
after its betrayal, its long disappearance
I do not trust the sun
never knowing how the day will turn
from sun to suddenly lashing out
hail and rain or simply withdrawing its warmth
before dying at the end of the day
while others step, dressed out in flimsy petals
I prickle and sweat beneath protective layers
I cannot quite discard.

Dawn Chorus

NL Whiteley

Disgruntled awake
while my lovely, sweet, charming, cherished partner
snores great honking snorts

A Study of Anguish

Morag Anderson

Spring, fool dark seeds to burst with abandon,
etch me in fern fronds of opaline frost,
quicken the riddle of first-light birdsong,
velvet me naive in Swan's-neck Thyme-moss.
Rouse the river's copper rocks with snowmelt,
set-square the bone-grey sky with Svalbard geese,
crown granite corries with morning's lilac,
souse me under clouds of blackthorn's promise.

First, free me of the blade in winter's eye
that switches my skin with willow branches,
slices thin days from the shank of long nights.
Remember me as the season passes –
drunk on the ruby bloom of squandered days,
sweetly debauched by the forest's decay.

My Best Friend

Catherine McKinlay

You're the always-burning
scented candle on my desk

You're that constant trace of
peppermint or lavender

You bring calm even when
I don't know I can smell you

Shape and Movement

the Abhainn Shira lay,
like a bored child's ribbon
discarded wanton
on a russet carpet

Martin Goldie, *Abhainn Shira*

Dance of the Midges

Nikita Parik

Lying skywards on a wooded bench
by the loch, eyes
looking up

at an evening descending,
an explosion of ebony
forming & unforming galaxies

in shifting spirals: now a DNA
now a bird's nest, now the shape
of a serpentine river

that flows through this city,
until a sharp wind breaks the illusion,
blows them away, takes them

back into the depths of the woods,
those crafty, artsy buggers.

Threat of the Urban Reds

Beth McDonough

Forget whatever you remember of Tufty.
We never joined his Club.
Shove off your notions
of some fucking Nutkin
and all his puny bunch.

Ask our colourless cousins.
The line is drawn at Campy:
we have paid Park Rangers trap them.
Then they feed the end of their lacklustre lives
to unfussy wolves in the children's zoo.

We are the only Urban Reds.
Dundee through and through. Our gang.

*Dundee is home to the only known urban population of red
squirrels. Camperdown Park is at the edge of their habitat.*

Little Poems

Donald Saunders

'Lyric' – the little word has wings
And warbles as it flies.
No others from the Muses' clutch
Approach its melodies.

The bravest of the brood is fledged
And fain to leave the nest.
Go, my pretty one, take wing,
Fly North, South, East and West!

Alas! It flies too high to hear;
Its message from afar
A long white streak of shit to smear
The windscreen of your car.

But No Ladies

Annie Sturgeon

Long slim legs
in pink stockings;
but no ladies –

webbed-footed fishwives
down by the docks
arms a-flap.

Screeching, 'queue, queue, queue!'
But none of them do.

Scavenging, squabbling,
pilfering, plundering,
raucous;
glaucous.

Chips with everything.

Rising Skylark Sings

Annie Sturgeon

Twa corbies devaul
Tae pluck een frae a deid yow
Risin lav'rock lilts

Two young crows descend
To pluck eyes from a dead ewe
Rising skylark sings

Cardinal Wooing

Salvatore Difalco

Disparities in beauty aside, we find enchantment under our hammered tin canopy sipping Dubonnet on the rocks and beholding the clever hopping and parry-thrust flashes of that red so particular to this brilliant entity. Look at him performing daring aeronautical maneuvers between chimneys and clotheslines without a pilot's license. He's doing what he can to turn on the hen, risking life and wing. Personally, I'm impressed. Meanwhile Frank Sinatra's laughing along with the crowd between tunes on Radio Deluxe. I turned you on to jazz, remember? Can't remember if you dig Sinatra, but even his laughter seems perfectly phrased. Recorded in New York City circa 1959. You shake your ice cubes for a refill. I aim to please, my love, as does the little red dude, trying to feed his gal seeds beak-to-beak. Then Ella croons the Wedding Song which seems so perfect I bust a gut laughing and you follow suit, hiding your new front teeth – you fell face first a month ago on the path stones – and scare the wan female into the boughs of the grand old oak behind the apple trees, leaving the red suer puzzled and furiously tweeting.

Last Sleepy Half Thoughts Before Sleep

Bruach Mhor

Are they thoughts at all, floating by
      like ghosts of dandelion heads?
  Or flotsam
       not quite landing on your beach?

They don't pretend to make much sense
      (tails without bodies,
         hanging in the air),
   mumbling in the language
       of holes of cheese.

     Or dangling from a question mark.
Or starting somewhere very far away
    before concluding
       in the nowhere pillow.   B.E.D.

How to Call Geese

Paulette Dubé

use equal amounts moose velvet, sky and elk bugle
mix thoroughly against rough autumn wind
fling upwards in a clockwise motion, as the moon sets

Hivernal (Winter in Montreal)

Alison Roe

On a winter window,
icy ferns
unfurling.

Morning snow.
Flakes of light
falling from the sun.

A perfect and pristine day,
diamond dust
blowing past the glass.

Coffee, croissant,
coffee, croissant,
snow.

Haiku for Hire

Michael McGill

A Glasgow taxi
gliding on the River Clyde...
£5.00 – frostbitten.

Cause and Effect

Andy Raffan

Carol sat forward in the driver's seat, chin resting on her folded arms, hugging the steering wheel. She watched the raindrops make slow slaloms down the windscreen. Slimy orange sparkles from the streetlights outside the surgery. Did they have any notion of randomness as they navigated their way down? Of the malignant force of the wiper blades waiting to slice them apart. Would they change course if they could know? Do something different?

She jerked upright. A whuff of chilled air and dampness blasted her as Steve dived into the passenger seat.

'What did they say then?' he said, rubbing his hands together.

'Nothing conclusive,' replied Carol, looking straight ahead. 'Still need more tests.'

'Ach well, no news is good news eh? So, what shall we cook for dinner then?'

She paused. Thinking. Slaloming. Then turned to face him.

'How about takeaway? My treat. The kids'll love it'

'On a school night? That is living dangerously.' He laughed, throaty still from the cold air.

'Rock *and* roll,' she said, smiling as she looked forward once more.

Carol turned the key. The dashboard lit up. Music filled the dark space around them. She flicked the wiper control with a finger edge. Two black whips arced across the windscreen, flinging the shattered raindrops aside and outwards as she steered them into the growing darkness of the storm.

Abhainn Shira

Martin Goldie

East,
beyond Loch Dochart, far below,
the Abhainn Shira lay,
like a bored child's ribbon
discarded wanton
on a russet carpet.
Its silver glitter drew
my sleep-starved eyes,
blinking in the early morning sun,
to distant hills towering in hazy silhouette
above a tranquil pink-tinged loch,
like a herd of sleeping elephants.

Connection and Memory

They've lined my fingers,
filled my body with time

Darrell Petska, *Good Ol' Mom and Pop*

The Playground

Emily Tee

At break time, lunch time, PE
I listen to the school kids screech
lives lived at full volume
but not all
when I passed the school
there were two wee girls
between the green wire of the fence
and the fir trees edging the playground
spying on their classmates
pig-tailed heads bowed as they whispered
secret observations

future poets, I think to myself

Lost-and-Found

Sean McMenemy

When I was five my dad had an affair with an Irish woman.

He packed a bag one night and said he was leaving for good. Left his keys on the kitchen table and took a taxi to the airport. My mum sat in there all night staring at the keys and crying. I didn't know it at the time and never would have, but my mum told me one night, for some reason, years after he died.

What I do remember was getting up for school that morning and finding him asleep at the front door, his bag like a pillow under his head. I kicked him in the leg and woke him, asked him why he was sleeping out there instead of inside. It's funny how you remember the wee things your parents say. He said he'd got lost.

Child

Allan Gaw

A child in blue sprints full tilt
and barefoot along the sunburnt sand.

He and his short shadow are both chased
by the same need to outrun the summer breeze.

With the last of his breath, he calls
to the dog leaping in the shallows.

The sea-soaked hound ups its ears and runs to him,
hurdling the waves, making for the shore.

Half-startled, he squeals as the dog twists,
wringing the salt-water from its coat,
drenching him in half-delight.

The boy's high-pitched giggle draws all our smiles,
parents, strangers
and poets alike.

Paper Crowns

Claire Reynolds

We had disliked one another intensely at first. Well, as intensely as a three-year-old can hate something, which on reflection is quite a lot. There're no half measures when you're three. Kimberly locked me in her attic and in retaliation I rubbed her face in a handful of Laburnum; its golden, sugar-puffed pods a potent poison. We duelled like this for a short while before realising we were two sides of the one coin.

Our gardens backed on to one another, separated by a wooden fence so enveloped by hawthorn that the two were indistinguishable. From May the May bloomed white, and we'd tape it onto crudely made paper crowns. As we approached double figures we biked everywhere, casting our net more widely, discovering new places to hide and seek; where huge beech trees held and shaded us, or scuffed and splintered us if disrespected.

In the summer of 1995, we were fifteen. For the first time Kimberly holidayed with us. Journeying to Kent in the car my parents played Neil Diamond and The Kinks. Kimberly relished the music my parents played, our day trips, the food we ate. She'd look at me in horror if I disrespected my parents, but I yearned for pints of shandy in her back garden, a Chinese take-away, free rein in Tammy Girl. Not Laura Ashley, Café Gandolfi and elbows off the table.

Arriving in Hythe we ran to the beach the way you do when you're caught between girl and woman. Well, at least I did; loose limbed yet self-conscious about bits that newly jiggled. I jumped onto the shingle from the sea wall awkwardly, while Kimberly touched down like she'd parachuted in on silk. The sun had been baking the shallows all day and we paddled, progressing to a wade as we saw off the outgoing tide. Kimberly smacked water towards me with her hand, and I clasped my hands together and pumped a jet that landed on her shorts, she shrieked, then pondered, 'I've never been to a chuckie beach, there's millions of them, wonder how they even got here?'

'They're pebbles. It's a shingle beach.'

'Chuuuckies! Chuuuuuckies!' she sang, so loud and Glasgow.

I met her eyes and added my own line.

'Big wans, wee wans, pink wans, white wans!'

We raved in the water, dancing in circles, two wild things singing our new anthem. We couldn't stand for laughing, so bobbed on our backs holding hands, like sea otters cast adrift for a while. When we stood, a group of boys were shielding squinting eyes from the sun, staring at us from the shoreline.

'They think we're mermaids!' Kimberly mocked in an English accent.

The next few weeks were campfires, cider, kisses on the beach. Milestones that left us with proper secrets to share. To compare it to a marriage would be to say it was the honeymoon period. The very best of days, bathed in sunlight. No half measures.

A Teenage New Year in Wales

Jim Lloyd

The four of us in John Hilton's Morris Traveller – heading north on the M6. What I remember is that after the blowout we went up the embankment and back down, spinning, to end up stalled and facing the wrong way in the fast lane. John restarted the car – moved it to the hard shoulder and changed the wheel. We stopped in the next service station – somehow not too perturbed. How we managed to avoid being hit is something of a mystery to me now.

We camped at Willy's Farm with its very basic amenities, and someone stole the Christmas pudding from our tent. The next day we climbed Tryfan and the Glyders in snow and ice. Afterwards, we played pool in the Vynol Arms at Nant Peris with Freddie Mercury on the jukebox. Mick didn't get into a fight with the locals. He always added a certain frisson to any social gathering. How we managed to avoid getting hit is something of a mystery to me now.

Send Me a Postcard

Eileen Farrelly

Send me impossible blue skies
over beaches with bright rugs laid out
like the fortune teller's scattered deck.
Make me laugh at old fashioned
seaside humour – all bums 'n' tits
and knotted hankies. Or keep it clean:
pristine snow-capped peaks.
Show me the wildlife,
the high life, the low life.
Take your pick from the revolving stand
just as long as you write
Wish you were here

Things We Miss As Parents

Ben Banyard

First, the wakeful night feeds, all that milk,
the feverish sterilisation, the cracked skin on your hands.

Nappies, full of all sorts, sagging around waists,
the suspicious whiffs which grown-ups pretend not to notice.

Getting them down for afternoon naps,
driving mile upon mile, the memory maps
we draw as we motor aimlessly with rear view glances.

The hours spent coaxing out those first words,
Mamma, Dadda, names to sketch their narrow horizon
and then all at once they babble endlessly, verbal scribble.

I dread the time when I reach behind me as I cross a road,
saying *hand? hand?* assuming there will be a tiny complicit paw,
the jogging weight of steps to keep up,
only to find I'm standing there alone.

Good Ol' Mom and Pop

Darrell Petska

Inveterate travelers now,
yet returning on a whim
to creak the loose stair,
clink the cupboard's dish.

It's no longer what they say,
but what they don't,
their silence eloquent as stars,
breezy as summer leaves.

They've lined my fingers,
filled my body with time.
Everywhere they're not,
I feel them hovering there.

Nae Sae Different

Eilidh Crofton

Ken at feeling? Whin ye huv the *perfect buzz* n ye can feel yersel sobering up, and in at moment there's no a bigger tragedy in the wurld. Aye, so ats where we wis. We huv a small and precious windae tae redeem the situation.

We're steppin intae the big shop, men oan a mission, bit its sae bright ah cannae hink proper.

We load up fur the gaff; I grab the biggest cake ah can find – Latvians eywis bring fine pieces to yer gaff. It's wan o their best qualities.

It aw clinks ontae the conveyor belt waking the hail shoap, they're gye silent creatures here, see. A vicious glower lights up in oor direction, and the maist crabbit, haggard, auld wifey barks at us from her lair. Oor blank stares at her yells in Latvian only encourage her tae screech higher, and afore the windows smash I interrupt, offering Russian as a conversational olive branch.

'Shit-toe?' Ah try.

'Knees-leesya alkogol posty-ah deen-avsat-ohva!'

Awwww shite. Ah sober up like a deer under polis headlamps. They dinnae sell alcohol efter 10! Ah should really ken better, being frae Scotland an aw.

I ask politely if she can sell us any 'Tabaccy?' and add a few 'pa-sha-loo-staas' fur good measure.

Similar guttural screeches emerge frae the mooth o the beast. The yells are somehow mair terrifying whin I mind fit she's sayin. I repeat masel and she crescendos intae a full out bellow – am feart she's gonny swing fur us. I kin hear the click-clack o her cloven hoofs hidden under the swivel chair.

Against aw ma ain interests, I ask again, kenning fine weel at there's a selection o every kindy baccy yu cuid wish fur right behind her. Nae chance. If she's winting tae gerd her treasure like a dragun, then fine. Am trying tae quit onywey.

The three o us stumble ootside, fine piece in haun, n nuttin else. Unscathed, or there aboots, jist a few wee scorch marks frae the dragun's breath. Doubled over in the smurr and the snaw, we cannae stop laughing.

'It's like they kent we was coming! Sending us a quine straight over fae Aiberdeen!'

Japanese Visitor

Charlie Gracie

He was surprised we remembered
every year
Hiroshima, Nagasaki.

His home in Sendai, 100 kilometres from Fukushima Daiichi
his wife and children there with him
when it all went to fuck.
We were lucky, he said, with the wind.

100 kilometres.
Here to the Heads of Ayr
where I watched gannets that time
scythe the sea.

Time

Katy Ewing

I'm using A.I.
to colourise old photos,
my late dad as a toddler, suddenly
his knitted jersey and underpants
made of coloured wool,
not just a texture of greys,
his curls golden, his cheeky smile brought alive

and maybe even more astonishing,
the lawn and hedges green and living,
lifted through time from eighty-five years past.

Transformation and Belief

I lurked under the shadow of trees, crouched amongst the brambles, let their sweet sharpness prickle my tongue. A grown woman, beckoning fairies and ghouls.

Ellen Forkin, *A Trick of the Dappled Light*

Blossoming

Janet Crawford

When the licht lay low on fields
I'd tae staund richt near tae count yer segments
each wan sae ticht wrapped
it looked like it was haudin oan tae the dark
as if tae say no yet
no yet

That same licht wid stay tae guide the moon
tae tak its place tae mornin came
when it wid dae the same again

Saein tae ony brave enough tae search
that it ae believed they'd draw the strength tae blossom
if they only sensed when hints o warmth and tiny rebirths
greeted mair than gorse petals opening
in the gloom o a January morning.

Bluebells

Ian McDonough

The bluebells are out
spotting the wood
like a beautiful plague.

And this little stream
has spent
all its winter water.

What happened to my days?
In hunting glory
I missed
that they were running,
bright and sparkling,
through my outstretched hands.

But the bluebells are out
spotting the wood
like a beautiful plague.

A Trick of the Dappled Light

Ellen Forkin

I wanted to believe in something. Ghosts. Dragons. Will-o-the-wisps. I stood at the edge of the forest, peered into the dark and deep. I trod through derelict houses, touched their decay. I counted the standing stones, once, twice, waiting for lightning to strike. An unearthly chill. A glimpse of the unknown.

The woods were my constant haunt, with its stream trickling, twisting on and on. A sun-dappled day, I whistled a joyless tune. A jay startled. I lurked under the shadow of trees, crouched amongst the brambles, let their sweet sharpness prickle my tongue. A grown woman, beckoning fairies and ghouls.

And yet.

I listened. The softest hush of leaf against leaf in the treetops. And something other. I stood at the stream's edge, straining to hear the strange humming over its rush and chatter. There! Where the water bows around the ash: a bent-back figure. Hunched amongst the shining pebbles, nose to water, a woman washing bloody garments with strong, clenched fists.

'Bean-nighe.'

She paused, looked at me with small, mournful eyes. Hummed her solemn song. I shuddered; a violent tremor. But. Fairies and ghouls: no such thing. I turned away from the foreteller of death. A trick of the dappled light. I would watch telly, eat dinner, phone my mother. I would survive the day, the night, on and on.

All I had to do was not believe.

When Death Comes Calling

Lyndsey Croal

When Death came to call, I was planting flower bulbs in the garden. There was a strange whistling sound before their descent. Like an arrow piercing the air. Then, Death landed with a thud on the newly unearthed soil. A moan of something like pain. A wing askew and broken.

Death looked at me, hollow-eyed and weary. Skeletal fingers grasped a handful of earth and it trailed from their hand like sand from an hourglass.

'It's not my time,' I said.

Death didn't reply, only touched their broken wing, head tilted to one side, as if confused or disoriented.

I stood up, offered my hand. 'Come inside, let me help.'

*

Death stayed for three days while I nursed them back to health. Though they didn't speak, their presence was oddly comforting. Familiar, like an old friend. I told them about my life, my family. The ones that had already left me. The ones that hadn't. The good I'd done. The mistakes I'd made. The dreams I still had.

Death didn't judge. Only listened. While they rested, I carried on my day-to-day – called on friends and family, then finished planting my flowerbed. New life would bloom in Spring.

On the fourth morning, I found Death by the window, wings outstretched. Sunrays illuminated them in an ethereal glow. They reached out a hand.

But I stepped away. 'It's not my time,' I said, again.

Death lowered their head, solemn. For a moment, I thought they'd fly towards me, take me in those skeletal arms, and soar back up into the sky. But then with a flutter of wings, they flew from the window and disappeared into the cold grey morning.

*

Some years later, Death returned. They didn't fall from the sky this time, merely appeared by my window with the birdsong at dawn, as I lay half-asleep in bed. They looked different – their face had changed. More solid, less featureless, almost a reflection of my own. And I realised why back then they had seemed so familiar. Why we had been able to sit like old friends.

When they approached my bed and reached out their hand, I took it this time. A scratch began at my shoulders. Baby feathers bristled.

When Death came to call for the second time, I was ready. Together, we left the world as equals – wings new and unbroken.

Takeaway Mourning

John Tinney

We keep a corpse oan display in a bedroom and expect tae get a good night's sleep wance the coffin's gone. Is it any wonder we think every fart of noise is evidence ae the supernatural?

'Hurry up and stoap hiding aw the time,' ma granda says. 'Go see yir ma and pey your respects before somebody else snuffs it.'

Who ordered wan deid mother in a coffin and a sausage supper!

It's no really the time tae imagine a funeral director functions like a busy chippy, but needs must when there's a dead imposter ae your maw in a box. Ah widnae wish this oan ma worst enemy, never mind ma maw, and aw that eulogy pish is actually true for her. Aye, everybody lights up a room wance they're deid. It must just be me that remembers them being withoot redeeming features.

Salt and vinegar oan the coffin or just the sausage supper?

'Don't start bawling like a wee lassie,' ma granda says. 'You need tae be strong. You need tae behave like a man.'

Ah need tae be a man at thirteen years of age and no cry for ma deid mother. Right ye are, ya prick. How am ah no supposed tae cry? Ah'm human, weak and saddled wae this elite level wanker till ah can get a proper joab. Ah widnae trust ma granda tae raise a hand withoot fuckin it up, and noo he's raising me.

Is your mother wanting a pickle wae her sausage supper?

'Thanks very much, Ma,' ah tell her eftir ma granda leaves us be. 'You could've hung oan till ah wis a wee bit aulder and could get a joab.' Ah look at her face fir the last time and allow maself a few seconds tae let go before tightening the lid oan the jar and wiping away any evidence of failing tae be a so-called man again.

Erosion

Andy Raffan

Boy sits zigzagged on the riverbank
worn out trainers jiggling over rippling surface.
Tracksuit legs parallel daddy's long legs,
between them rod and line a patient perpendicular.
He thinks of angles – angling –
the beaten obtuseness of grownups
their sharp reflexive answers
acutely narrowed horizons.

But here they soften by degrees
as the words cast out their lines –
of living in the woods off fire-smoked fish
a never going home time, a forever here time;
the man and the boy and the endless water
and the smoothing of the edges.

For Sale: Childhood Memories

Liane McKay

Mixed bundle including (but not limited to) rainy holidays,
school parents' nights, first kiss. Middle child, no family pets,
distant father

Would interest collectors and curious alike

Selling as lot, needs gone ASAP

£40 ono. Swaps considered

Cash or Card?

Karen Arnold

Her shop is set out in the pool of light from the standard lamp. She is dressed in Harry Potter pyjamas and a green and black witches' hat from the dressing up box. Still warm and pink flushed from bath time. She has set out her stall on an upturned box; acorns and seashells for money, an old biscuit tin for a cash register.

Heavy weather has been brewing all afternoon. Now a storm cat is howling and prowling around our cottage, scratching at the windows, hungry and furious. Fingernails of rain scrape and tap at the glass, and I know that in the morning the beach will have changed shape completely.

'It's a witches' shop, Daddy! I'm selling spells and potions.'

I am only half listening. I have only been half there since we heard the maroon go off an hour ago, her mother's mobile ringing only a split-second after with the call to the lifeboat station. From the corner of my eye, I can still see her flashing past us, a blur of black curls and yellow oil skin, waving, yelling instructions about supper and bedtime, and she won't be late and don't worry.

Don't worry.

The clock ticks on. The radio murmurs away in the background. The shipping forecast. Ironic.

'What would you like to buy from my shop, Daddy?'

I'm pulled back into the room by her insistent sand piper voice. Playing for time, I ask what she has for sale. She sweeps a hand across the display. I see it properly this time, the gleanings from our afternoon strand loping along the beach and the cliff edge as the sky darkened and the seabirds streamed towards land, away from what was coming. There is a hag stone, strands of seaweed woven through the hole. A piece of sea glass, misty and smooth, tied to a gull feather with bright orange nylon rope. A tiny, bleached crab shell sitting in the green glass bottle, stoppered with a bunch of sea holly. I remembered that she had been so determined to pick it, ignoring the prickly leaves that drew blood from her fingertips.

'I've made spells! Good luck charms, you can buy one for Mummy.'

Caught by the reflex of reassurance, I start to say that Mummy doesn't need good luck, but her brown eyes are fixed on mine and the words remain unspoken. Play the game. Play the game.

I point to the crab bottle, an old, old part of me knowing without thinking that blood magic is strong magic.

'Excellent choice, sir.' She mimics a shop keeper's patter perfectly. 'Will that be cash or card?'

There is a knock at the door.

A Sting in the Tale

Kate Leimer

'Pssst!'

My heart sank. Someone had found me. I'd left the others packing up camp, hoping to escape the tourist chatter for five minutes on my own. Surely not much to ask: a little uninterrupted contemplation of the awe-inspiring scenery, to enjoy the silence with a cool breath of wind stroking my face. My chance to feel like Aragorn, striding alone across the empty landscape; a warrior-explorer, ready for anything.

I'd probably been reading too much Tolkien again.

'Hello? Can I help you?'

'It's a bit awkward.' The voice resonated, as if the speaker were in a vast cavern. Looking round, I could see only scattered boulders and grassy paths. No obvious caves. 'Up here!'

I raised my gaze to a deep fissure in the rock.

'Don't be scared,' the voice said.

'Fine.' I folded my arms. 'I'm not scared. Now what's all this about? We're on a schedule and I can't hold the others up. What's the matter? Are you stuck?'

'In a manner of speaking.'

'Right. Stay there. I'll give you a hand.' Pulling myself up about seven feet of almost sheer rock, I braced myself on a narrow ledge. A man's face appeared, followed by his naked shoulders and arms.

There was no sign he was stuck. I edged away. The rest of him began to appear.

'Oh what?! Seriously? Are those your legs? All of them? And what the hell is that? No way; is this a joke? Are you real? You can't be! What happened? Is it like that film, *The Fly*? A scientific experiment gone wrong? Get away from me!'

I shuffled off the ledge to land in an undignified heap on my backside, looking up at a man who was human as far as the waist and from there on, a scorpion, including a vicious-looking tail waving about under no apparent control.

I scrambled backwards, my feet showering chitinous, jointed legs with dust and pebbles as he descended onto the path and leaned over me.

'I'm sorry! I didn't mean to startle you!'

I glared up at him.

'You didn't mean to *startle* me! What do you do when you do want to startle people? Jump out of a cake at children's parties?'

'I am Aqrabuamelu. I warn travellers of danger. Wait, please,' he said, as I scrambled to my feet, 'I must warn you! About your boyfriend. He's planning to kill you.'

'What?'

'You are Shamash. Justice. Light. I am here to guard you.'

'No, I'm Sharon. I'm a legal secretary, from Pinnor.'

'Oh. Bugger.' He began edging back towards the rockface. 'Sorry. Bit out of practice. But be careful, won't you? Danger lies ahead. Don't go into the darkness.'

His voice faded as he folded his immense height in half, disappearing into the rock, leaving only the sound of the wind, whispering across the grass and the scream of a bird of prey, high above.

Later:

'Dave? Um, that caving trip tomorrow; do you mind if I don't come along?'

Months Go By

Liane McKay

How odd: my old town
got cold.
No drops of gold bloom.
Moths on mossy schoolbooks.
Old postbox, hollow.
Words lost.
Worlds known only to folk songs, now.
No knobbly rocks.
Stony knoll grown smooth,
worn down from boots.
Shoots trod,
tomorrow's blossom, lost.
No cost. Nobody's sorry.
Nobody looks fondly
on my old town.
No – *don't*.
Don't stop now; go on.
Don't grow roots.
Don't hold on, for so long,
to old town ghosts.

The Stacks

Scott Montgomery

'Watch out for any ghosts!' smirks Jenny, the librarian.

Apart from a casual-staff induction day a few months back, I have never set foot in Library HQ. It was built in the late Victorian era, with a red sandstone exterior and domed ceiling. I am tasked with going down to the Closed Stacks (unavailable to the general public) to retrieve some customer requests for the next day.

Clutching a plastic storage box and a printed list of wanted books; I descend into the dimly-lit basement. My footsteps echo as I pass a couple of old mahogany desks with the usual library detritus on them – pencils, adhesive labels, stamps, ink pads and binding materials. Amongst the clutter there is also an old portable transistor radio. Nowadays there is a market for 'retro' facsimiles of that type of electronic kit but this one looks authentic – perhaps an antique from the 1960s.

I find the first few items on my list. One is on a higher shelf and I must use a ladder to reach the book. I jolt in surprise as I hear a sharp 'plinking' sound beneath me. I almost lose my grip and look down – realising that it is only a pencil rolling off the desk and bouncing to the ground. I descend, knowing that I was lucky not to have fallen.

Back to my list. Then, there is a torrent of ear-splitting noise. It lasts for about twenty seconds then stops as abruptly as it starts.

Have I tripped some kind of alarm?

Then the racket starts again. No, not an alarm – there's no distinct pattern.

High pitched screeching at first, then hissing, before an eruption into some kind of weird burbling; a distorted cacophony of –

what, exactly? I swear it sounds like the babble of human voices. There's something vaguely familiar about it; wildly oscillating between unsettling low registers then high ones, no rhyme or reason.

Like... a *radio* changing channels?

Feeling increasingly spooked, I run over to the desk area. I am still alone – but the vintage radio is blaring loudly. The front panel is lit up; the needle on the main dial is going haywire – back and forth like it's... alive.

'If this is a joke I don't find it funny!' I shout out to no one.

Dropping the storage box, I cover my ears, trying to drown out the horrible noise. Grasping the wretched radio I attempt to switch it off but to no avail. Angry, I throw the contraption to the hard stone floor with an echoing clatter. Some components detach themselves; the back panel comes off and a metal circuit board goes flying.

Quiet. Earlier I had foolishly thought the silence was unsettling.

Picking up the pieces of the transistor, I try to put the back panel back on – and realise that the radio itself *has no batteries in it.*

I cobble the bits back together as best I can with trembling hands and shove the infernal thing back on the desk. Then I set about retrieving the remaining books I came for and dash back upstairs.

I consider telling Jenny what happened but don't want her to think I'm mad.

Back at the issuing desk computer terminal, out of curiosity I search online for any unusual local goings-on. In 1961, a library custodian, Gilbert Briggs died in an accident. Apparently he fell from a ladder in the basement of this very building. He was a keen radio enthusiast.

Ghost in the Machine

Hilary Ayshford

My washing machine is haunted.

Two months ago one of my husband's black socks went missing. That in itself is not unusual, but since he is a creature of habit and always buys the same brand and colour it never takes long for a stray to find a new partner. The strange thing this time was the presence of the intruder – a single sock, jauntily striped in shades of lime, emerald and olive. I stowed it at the back of his sock drawer, on the basis that the other one might turn up at some point.

A week later it was a pair of purple boxer shorts. Kenneth is a navy briefs man all the way; he says boxers make him feel insecure. I tucked them away in a pile of my jumpers in case he found them and started asking awkward questions – unlikely, but there's a first time for everything.

Next, an alien shirt arrived. Not in the pastel colours that my husband favours, but a daring dark blue and red stripe with a contrasting white collar. The kind of shirt he wouldn't be seen dead wearing. That one I secreted at the back of the airing cupboard – after I'd ironed it, of course – ready for the next trip to the charity shop.

Then the washing machine started turning itself on in the middle of the night. I came down to a kitchen full of warm steam and a pair of damp slim-fit jeans in the drum. I unplugged the machine and turned off the water supply.

It made no difference.

I lay in bed that night listening to the machine waltz its way around the kitchen, bumping into the table on its way to the back door. The crashing and thumping of its escape bid drowned out the sound of Kenneth's snoring. He slept soundly, oblivious, but in the morning he looked washed out. His hair was losing its colour, and his skin was grey and wrinkled.

For the rest of that week random items continued to turn up, including a teeshirt the colour of cinder toffee, size medium, and the other green-striped sock.

My husband was shrinking. His clothes seemed to fit more loosely, and he was as tense and uptight as a cashmere sweater washed at 90 degrees for an hour.

Yesterday morning, there was a damp spot by his side of the bed and a trail of drips leading along the landing, down the stairs and into the kitchen. Kenneth looked like the pale patch on a duvet cover bleached by the sun, as though all the colour had been leached out of him.

Today when I got up a stranger was making breakfast in the kitchen, dressed in a dark orange teeshirt, slim-fit jeans and stripy green socks. There was a dark cavity under the worktop like a missing tooth.

Wherever the washing machine has gone, Kenneth appears to have gone with it. I don't think I'll be replacing them.

Gorleston Gulls

Laura Lewis-Waters

Beside morning spume
they dance to shipping forecasts
knowing there is more

Sunweys and Widdershins

Hilary Coyne

'The days are repeating.'

The woman was hanging the damp, stringy washing on the whirligig, back turned to the dark clouds on the horizon.

'What's that?' I had intended just to carry on past but I can't ignore a greeting when I'm on my own.

'I did exactly this same day yesterday.'

'They say it often feels that way.'

She sighed. 'No, I mean the days are actually repeating. Look at this…' She spun the whirligig half a turn to the right and held up a child's once-white vest. 'That was a raspberry stain this morning. I washed the same mark yesterday. And the day before.'

'Isn't that just life with small children? All the days seem the same.'

'It looks like a bird every time.'

'The stain looks like a bird?' I cocked my head and squinted at the mark.

'Yes.' She spun the gig again and started on the next section. Still ignoring the clouds.

'If this day were repeating, wouldn't we have had this conversation before?'

'We have.' She sounded weary. 'You're about to tell me it's going to rain.'

I swallowed down the warning. 'And then what happens?'

'Tomorrow we'll do this all again.'

'When did all this start?' I wondered if she knew.

'It started when we cleared the garden. You came by the day we felled the big oak to make this drying space.'

I nodded. I'd been travelling alone that day too and the sight of the old tree lying on its side had shocked me into stopping. I had known then there'd be consequences.

'I've regretted it ever since. We upset the balance of things; the children are afraid to come out here and the hens won't lay.'

She looked bone tired. Not surprising with three little ones but someone needed to keep an eye, prevent further mischief.

A chattering in the trees drew my attention.

'I should –'

'You need to get going.'

'Yes, they're waiting for me.'

'I know.' Her voice was flat.

She picked up the empty laundry basket and with her left hand gave the washing a last whirl. She frowned through the grey blur, her body sagging like a wrung-out cloth.

Something had to change. Our ways can be inflexible but this could yet be undone.

'*Widdershins,*' I called to her, savouring the sound of the old word.

She looked up, startled. 'What?'

'You always spin it *widdershins*. The other way is *sunweys*.' A thought tickled me. 'Might even be better for the washing!'

For a moment she was still, staring at me as though she'd just understood something, then she reached forward and spun the dryer with her right hand. The damp clothes flared limply but the air around the whirligig flexed like the surface of a pond.

The shadows on the grass flickered and she looked up at the thin needles of watery sunlight now piercing the cloud.

A smile found her mouth and she turned to thank me but I had already flown.

Acknowledgements

My gratitude goes to all the authors who contributed their words to this anthology.

A big thanks to Joanna Helms for their listening ear and gentle encouragement when I didn't realise I needed it.

Finally, thanks to anyone who has supported Soor Ploom Press by subscribing to the newsletter, spreading the word about us, or buying our books.

Author biographies

Alison Roe is from Edinburgh, lived in Montreal for ten years, and now lives in the North West Highlands where she walks, writes, rows, plays taiko and flits around in her wee Japanese van. Her writings wash up intermittently at solanoire.com.

Allan Gaw is a pathologist by training, writer by inclination. In 2022, he won the UK Classical Association Creative Writing Competition and the International Alpine Fellowship Writing Prize. His debut poetry collection, *Love & Other Diseases* was published in 2023 by Seahorse Publications.

Andy Raffan is a member of Strathkelvin Writers Group and was shortlisted for the Edinburgh Prize for Flash Fiction in 2022 and 2023. He had a short story featured in *New Writing Scotland* and his flash fiction and poetry has been published by Ink, Sweat and Tears and Soor Ploom Press.

Anjali Ramayya started writing two years ago, following retirement. Her work has been short/long listed in competitions and published in *Poetry Scotland, Propel, Dreich, Writers' Umbrella,* and *Ukraine – A World Anthology of Poems on War.*

Annie Sturgeon is an Aberdeenshire writer and artist who's had exhibitions and publications in a variety of places. She is currently writing more than painting.

Ben Banyard lives in Portishead, on the Severn Estuary just outside Bristol. His third collection, *Hi-Viz,* was published by Yaffle Press in 2021. Ben also edits *Black Nore Review,* an online journal of poetry and flash fiction.

Beth McDonough's poetry is widely anthologised. Her first solo pamphlet *Lamping for pickled fish* is published by 4Word and her site-specific poem has recently been installed on the Corbenic Poetry Path. She swims year round in the Tay, foraging close by.

Bruach Mhor is a fan of sea slugs. His poems have most recently appeared in such places as *Gutter, Dream Catcher, Black Box Manifold, The Interpreter's House, Streetcake,* various Dreich Press anthologies, *Short and Sweet* (Volume One), and *Kleksograph.*

Carol McKay is a writer from Glasgow who was recently appointed as the 2023 FWS Scriever, an honorary position working to promote and support prose writers in Scotland. Her most recent novel, *White Spirit,* was published by PotHole Press in 2022, with author royalties being donated to the Addison's Disease Self-Help Group.

Catherine McKinlay, an english teacher based in Glasgow, has always written but fell in love with writing poetry while studying English with Journalism and Creative Writing at Strathclyde University. Her work has previously been published in a few Scottish magazines.

Charlie Gracie grew up in Baillieston, Glasgow. His poetry collections, *Good Morning* (2010) and *Tales from the Dartry Mountains* (2020), were published by Diehard Press. His first novel, *To Live With What You Are* (2019), was published by Postbox Press. His most recent book, *Belfast to Baillieston*, was published in 2023 by Red Squirrel Press.

Claire Reynolds has an MLitt in Creative Writing from the University of Glasgow where she is currently undertaking her DFA. Her work can be found in *From Glasgow to Saturn* and *Gutter*, and she was recently shortlisted for the Bridport Prize in Flash Fiction.

Darrell Petska, a retired university editor, has published poetry and fiction in a wide range of periodicals. A father of five and grandfather of seven, he lives near Madison, Wisconsin, with his wife of more than 50 years.

Donald Saunders is a grumpy old man who lives in the Trossachs. He has been writing, mainly poetry, for over 50 years. Gosh.

Eileen Farrelly's poems have appeared in *Marble, Writers' Café Magazine* and in anthologies and her chapbook, *Some things I ought to throw away*, was published in 2021. She is also a songwriter and can be found singing for beer in various pubs around her hometown, Glasgow.

Eilidh Crofton is a student at the University of Glasgow currently living in Latvia's capital city, Riga. Experimenting with Scots and Doric has allowed Eilidh to simultaneously reflect on new experiences and feel closer to home.

Ellen Forkin is a chronically ill writer, living in windswept Orkney, with a love of folklore, myth and magic. Find out more at www.ellenforkin.co.uk.

Emily Tee used to work with numbers but switched to words. She's recently had some poems and flash fiction published. Originally from Northern Ireland, Emily now lives in England.

Helen Chambers won the Fish Short Fiction Prize in 2018, was nominated for Best Microfictions in 2019 and Pushcart in 2021. In summer 2023, she directed The Winter's Tale for the Wivenhoe Outdoor Shakespeare, and when not worrying how to stage 'exit pursued by bear,' she writes flash and short stories.

Hilary Ayshford is a former science journalist and editor now exploring the world of short fiction. She writes about anything and everything, from horror to humour, sci-fi to surreal, and has a penchant for the darker side of human nature.

Hilary Coyne is a Scottish writer of short stories and flash fiction. She was shortlisted for the Edinburgh Short Story Award 2023 and longlisted in the HWA Dorothy Dunnet Short Story Competition. Her work has been published by *Cranked Anvil, Glittery Literary, Fudoki Magazine* among others and can be found via hilarycoyne.com.

Ian McDonough is a poet and community worker based in Thurso. His most recent publication is *A Witch Among the Gooseberries* published by Mariscat.

Janet Crawford is a Falkirk-based writer and poetry film maker, with an interest in how we connect to each other and to nature in particular. Recent publications include *Razur Cuts, Nutmeg Magazine* and *Short and Sweet* (Volume One) from Soor Ploom Press.

Jenny Munro-Hunt is a writer of poetry and prose from Glasgow. Her work has been published in *The 6ress*, in *Heather: An Anthology of Scottish Writing and Art* (ed. Alice Louise Lannon) and her debut pamphlet will be published by the Black Cat Poetry Press in 2024.

Jim Lloyd is an artist and writer. He won a prize in the Rialto 'Nature and Place' poetry competition. His poems have appeared in *The Rialto, bind, Green Ink Poetry, One Hand Clapping Online, Presence Haiku Journal,* and *Wales Haiku Journal.* He lives in Northumberland, UK.

Joanna Helms was born in South Carolina and is now pre-settled (whatever that means) in Edinburgh. Previously a musician and educator, they currently work as an editor and occasional translator.

John Tinney is a Glaswegian writer. He has published fiction with *404 INK, Every Day Fiction, The Selkie, Razur Cuts* and others.

Karen Arnold is a writer and child psychotherapist living in Worcestershire.

Kate Leimer enjoys stories of all kinds and her writing has been published by *TL;DR Press, Idle Ink, Cabinet of Heed,* and *Cranked Anvil.* When not writing, she works in a library, surrounded by books, which makes her happy.

Katy Ewing is a writer and artist living in rural southwest Scotland. She has had poetry, prose and illustration published widely in magazines and anthologies including *New Writing Scotland, Gutter, Southlight, Zoomorphic* and *From Glasgow to Saturn,* and was winner of the Wigtown Poetry Competition's D&G Fresh Voice Award 2018.

Laura Lewis-Waters is a poet from the Midlands whose debut collection, *Bathroom Prisoners,* was published in 2022. Laura has also recently been published in *Free Verse Revolution Lit Magazine, Public Sector Poetry Journal* and *Streetcake Magazine,* and had a poem featured as part of the BBC Upload Festival 2022.

Lesley Jane Black works in the Higher Education sector and enjoys playing with language to evoke emotion and paint pictures in the mind. Her cat is keen on bedtime stories.

Liane McKay is a poet and editor of educational materials from Hamilton. Her work has appeared in magazines and anthologies across the UK.

Lyndsey Croal is an Edinburgh-based author of strange and speculative fiction, with work published in several magazines and anthologies. She's a Scottish Book Trust New Writers Awardee, British Fantasy Award Finalist, and a former Hawthornden Fellow. Her debut novelette *Have You Decided on Your Question* was published in 2023 with Shortwave Publishing. Read more of her work via www.lyndseycroal.co.uk.

Martin Goldie has been writing poetry for 3 years. He lives and works in Argyll and has been published in anthologies in the UK and abroad. His debut collection *Unshackled* was published in 2022 by Seahorse Publications and his poem *Awful Confusion* was shortlisted for the Janet Coats Memorial Prize 2023.

May Sharpe is based in the Cotswolds where she teaches in a primary school when not working on her 'whodunnit' novel.

Michael McGill is a poet from Edinburgh who has recently been published by *The Interpreter's House* and *Dreich*. His work has also recently appeared in *iamb* and the Scottish Poetry Library's *Poems by and for Social Workers* anthology.

Morag Anderson lives in Highland Perthshire and is the 2023 Federation of Writers (Scotland) Makar. Her debut pamphlet *Sin Is Due to Open in a Room Above Kitty's* is published by Fly On the Wall Press and the collaborative pamphlet *How Bright the Wings Drive Us* by Dreich.

Nikita Parik is the 2022–23 Charles Wallace Visiting Fellow at the University of Stirling. Her third and latest book, *My City is a Murder of Crows* (2022), was shortlisted for the Sahitya Akademi Yuva Puraskar and the Rabindranath Tagore Literary Prize.

NL Whiteley is an office manager from London who started writing during Covid lockdowns and hasn't stopped yet!

Paulette Dubé is a writer and photographer from Canada whose most recent collection of poems, *the deepest part of the river won't freeze*, was published by Green Olive Press in 2021.

Salvatore Difalco is the author of *Black Rabbit & Other Stories* (Anvil). His piece *Before the spaghetti hit the wall* was published in Volume One of *Short and Sweet*.

Scott Montgomery, author of the *2000 AD Encyclopedia* and with a story recently published in *The People's Friend*, has been a journalist, comic script writer and comedy writer since 1994.

Sean McMenemy was born in Paisley in 1988. An ex-footballer, barber, and taxi driver, he took up writing a few years ago. His stories have been published in *Southword*, *The Honest Ulsterman*, *thi wurd*, and *Creeping Expansions*.

Tavia Allan is a writer and lecturer based in London. She has work published in *Funny Pearls*, *The Hungry Ghost Project*, *Flash Fiction Magazine*, *MONO* and *Litro* among others. She often leaves the washing up in the hope a space-time rift will open in the kitchen overnight.

A note on Shannon Trust

Shannon Trust transforms lives by supporting disadvantaged people to learn to read.

A registered charity in England, Wales and Northern Ireland, each year they help thousands of people in prison to learn to read, so that they can build a different, more positive future for themselves and their families.

Shannon Trust's reading programme enables more people in prison to gain a fundamental skill that they need to navigate daily life. It provides prisoners with access to education, training and rehabilitative courses that will help them to address their offending, gain new skills and move into employment.

For thousands of people in prisons, and in the community, learning to read can completely transform their life.

Your purchase of this book helps to support Shannon Trust's vital work – £1 from the sale of each copy will be donated to the charity.

Learn more and support Shannon Trust by visiting their website at shannontrust.org.uk.